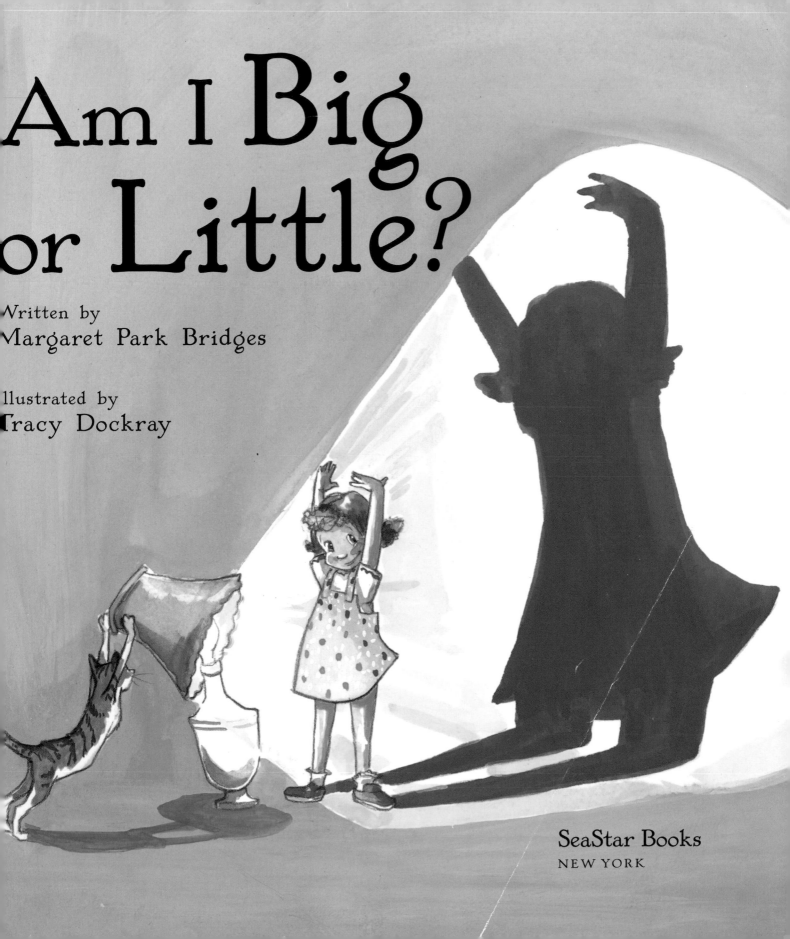

Am I Big or Little?

Written by
Margaret Park Bridges

Illustrated by
Tracy Dockray

SeaStar Books

NEW YORK

To Harriet,
for her support, generosity, and love
—M. P. B.

For Mark and Lily
—T. D.

First published in the United States by SEASTAR BOOKS,
a division of NORTH-SOUTH BOOKS, INC., New York.
Published simultaneously in Canada, Australia, and New Zealand by North-South Books,
an imprint of Nord-Süd Verlag AG, Gossau Zürich, Switzerland.
Library of Congress Cataloging-in-Publication Data is available.

The art for this book was prepared using watercolor and watercolor pencil.
The text for this book is set in 18-point Colwell.

ISBN 1-58717-019-1 (trade binding)
1 3 5 7 9 TB 10 8 6 4 2
ISBN 1-58717-020-5 (library binding)
1 3 5 7 9 LB 10 8 6 4 2

Printed by Proost N.V. in Belgium.

For more information about our books and the authors and artists who create them,
visit our web site: www.northsouth.com

Rise and shine, little one.

Time for big kids to wake up.

Mommy, am I **little** or am I **big?**

You're **both,** sweet pea.

But how can I be **big** and **little** at the same time?

Well,

you're littler than I am.

But I'm **bigger** than Kitty.

Right!

You're little enough
to crawl under your bed.

But I'm **big** enough to reach out and tickle you!

You're little enough
to ride piggyback
to the stairs.

But

I'm **big** enough

to h_{op}

all the way down.

You're little enough to bury
your face in Kitty's tummy.

But I'm **big** enough to carry him like a baby.

You're little enough to ride through the park in a stroller.

But I'm **big** enough to make the pigeons fly away!

You're little enough
to stand on my feet
while we *dance.*

But I'm **big** enough
to hold on tight
when you spin me!

You're little enough to have
a tea party under the kitchen table.

But I'm **big** enough to serve my guests *first*.

You're little enough
to want dessert
all day long.

But I'm **big** enough to wait for it.

You're little enough
to share your bath
with a fleet of boats.

But I'm **big** enough to be Captain!

You're little enough to **jump** on the bed.

But I'm **big** enough
to make it when I'm done.

You're little enough
to share a blanket with your animals.

But I'm **big** enough to save them from the dark.

You're little enough to pretend
you can *fly* to the moon.

But I'm **big** enough
to find my way home.

Well, I'm glad you're still little enough to sit in my lap.

I'm glad I'm **big** enough to wrap my arms around you!

Yes, sweet pea.
You're like a big present
in a little box.

A present for *you,* Mommy?

Of course—just what I *always* wanted!